KEŞKE

in Turkish, "keşke" (kesh-kay) expresses a wish or longing—
it can be roughly translated into English as "if only"

OTHER TITLES FROM AIRLIE PRESS

Keşke

Poems   JENNIFER A. REIMER

2022

Airlie Press is supported by book sales, by
contributions to the press from its supporters, and by
the work donated by all the poet-editors of the press.

P.O. Box 13325
Portland OR 97213
www.airliepress.org
email: airliepress@gmail.com

First Edition
ISBN 978-1-950404-08-7
Library of Congress record available at
https://lccn.loc.gov/2021952090

Printed in the United States of America
Cover and book design by N. Putens
Author photo by Patrick Hart
Cover artwork © Eylül Elitas Özmen

CONTENTS

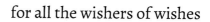

for all the wishers of wishes

Any fool can get into an ocean
But it takes a Goddess
To get out of one.

~ JACK SPICER

The siren and the sailor have both been me

~ CHARLIE ANNE

Keşke I.

start

    where

        —she—

    prophecy

remains

    fragment   :   stone

    pine   :   tressed

    coast   :   line

caves   — *Calypso,*

behind the azure window

    :   *the lovely goddess*

    the wanderer

driven time and again off

    course—

swept   a   way   *by wind and wave*

wide   wet   *wine-dark*

sea

the bewitching sea nymph
smiles at his

words "words words—"

with   holds   *stroking his arm*

water   line   with

draw   advance   withdraw

where   woven   chiaroscuro—

             ocean-
-tossed

     in   *her house*

cliff's dark crevasse—

this small space   widens

                   hours

to days   form
                  emerges
     as tidal rocks

     emerge—   *from goddess*

captive   captured

breeze   blows   *to storm*

beach   wrecked

        timber

           isle —

              "Be not deceived
                if I have veiled my look"

still   air   spins

epic   from   ruin

      — she —

scrawls   walls

hunts   history

      sings   *What a rascal you are*
                  with a devious mind
                  to think of speaking to me
      now

cast   net   cast   spell

      bind

all   wishes   to conceal

      cunning

    —she—

         swears—

—keşke—   *by this earth and the sky above*

this means the world

      O   *goddess-queen*

this is no

        beginning—

Keşke II.

—she— imprints

       bodies

on this extreme

      map

    wind-worn words—

     rocks—

balancing intention and hunger

    net sound of water

     net

nights softening sea—

      once the edge

some pull some path

    breathless
        still

mornings   —she—   wakes

      "you"

      lake   —she—

ocean—

      raised—

          rock—

all cartography and no touch

      offering

unnamed unspoken

      —keşke—

 as if we—   don't

          weave

as if wish would always

      sing to me, what's left

silence to song

      —she—

      longs

distant   letters

      the air—

softly through passageways

     and doors

          calling out to you

— she — reckons

     there's something called —

not quite
         slipping

beyond text
         beyond doubt   *for how else*

can we invoke

     struggle   afterworlds

without voice

light
    breath
         movement —

see : the objects   around

     drink   dark   residues

        absent
    inhale   names

     unspoken

the swallows of San Juan—

       return

            only

                what

—she—   leaves

       now   *I seem to find her, now*
       I   *realize she's far away*

watch: how

      this depends

      on—

      this

—mistake : wind for hair

linger long lay sleepless

      nights   sonneted—

—she— forest eyes

               green

                   coastline

    shored in sand,

                washed

    water drawing down

      gravity bent

          starlit

scan   body

          lines

do not
          alliterate
                    translate
                              belong—

          —she—

The Day After the Failed Military Coup

The day after the Failed Military Coup is hot. Everyone stayed up until
6 a.m. Bleary-eyed from live streaming Al Jazeera or BBC, we blinked into
the bright July. Some hours later, your body remembers: the sound and
feel of the Parliament explosion like the first plane first tower—another
hot day. Two days after the Failed Military Coup, you cry over 9/11 (at last).
The smoke and ash. The last train from lower Manhattan filled with
ghosts. The bodies falling through memory, always falling. Far away in
Anatolia, where summer smells like scorched sweet grass and pine, you
remember the smell of steel and death, how you walked past it twice a day
for months. On the day after the Failed Military Coup, you're still thinking
of *keşke* and feel guilty about this. You remember Andrew's first apartment
in the West Village in 2001 and you wish—(*keşke-keşke-keşke*). You talk
about poetry and—why you don't want to talk about it. On the day after
the Failed Military Coup, you drink because—. Turkey breaks—and you
don't want anyone to know. Two days after the Failed Military Coup, you've
decided, but you don't know it yet—   —and—   you might as well
finally—

Keşke III.

—she—

      descends

      river   valley

ancient Lycia

      way of—

          flowering
oleander
         fig
bay
     pine   wild

     grapevine

trails   maquis: mint, laurel, myrtle

     Timber Mountain   *Tahtalı Dağı*

—throne of gods—

                what were the right ways—
                what was the name that you gave her?
tumbled into wind
           —she—

—dreams   a hundred years

before

        Christ :

                the pirate chief Zenicetes

his kingdom lost

        So the pirate

     sets fire to his house   fiery Mt. Chimaera — *Yanartaş* —

—she—   imagines

     wife and daughters   *emerge from rock   burn*
                   inside—   *a flame that does not die by day or night*

part lion   part goat   part snake   Χίμαιρα

breath of—   female   fire   *enraged Anteia*

—she—   hybrid   *dishonored*

witness these details :   Mount Omurga :

       Çamoda Peak   winged   *Bellerophon who*

on all sides   arrowed   clouds   *broke the sacred bond between*

—she—   bewilders   *guest and host*

Zeus : his raging realm of

     female death :   she—

spits in the dirt   likes challenge

myth's   arterial   routes

           down

              the coast

      Çıralı   origin of—

Temple of Hephaestus   —

Burak, the TV actor

lights   a cigarette

       promises   *—keşke—*

into risen night—

—she—   reconfigures   *geography*

monstrous   goddess   *of attachment*

       combs   *snakes from her*

wet   cool   hair—   *one solid braid*

      —skin   *of sound—*

bruises to remember

      what   *might have been*

care

      what   *avoidance*   *plaited into desires not—*

      —she—

abandoned by—

        Olympos :

               : olives and dry oak

offer   aching *will*

        evidence   *you read*

                  what

     —she—

                  now reads—

Cave Wall

absent : landscape
where even this—
cave
tide-pulled
source material—
pock-marked cliff face
buried white

this is not a poem
about the moon
a stone set into
stone
or any number of days

in the visible terrain
of passing ships—
or her wrecked
wishes—
echo
locations
in silence

Keşke IV.

—she—
    swims in—

        visible worlds

matter :   common tongue   length

            of bay   leaves

                fallen

dry   pages   turn   margins to

letter   —she—   reads absence :

          a space you haven't yet filled

with   breath—   counts

four :

    one : *before you tumbl'd me*

    two : swallows nest

    three : *a document in madness*

    four : *you who long for things*

past   replica   pirate ship

wrecked   ruins   of—

             naming conventions :

    she dreams that she speaks
    the lines of the sea

deciphers   currents

               code :

that the view is more splendid

    if you would come
           four days

for   breath   space

we   have   made

    for more—

each   century   decoding

begins   again

    —she—

stars   skin

   seas   surface   lit

back   wards   against

incessant   click-clack

      water   and   air

                         constellate

—her body—   shell   wave   spray of foam

                   passage

through   time   gate

      way   cast   a—

way   ward   glance   a

way   word   spell   a

      way   out—

nothing   in   half

an emotion is   *—keşke—*

why   —she—   "must"   imagine—

    shadows   water

    through it   all
        ways

Keşke V.

she   —rituals—

           unknown

    inventions :
what
    our

             sadness—

says   most things

    happen

when—   wishes

margins   notes

not   "you"   not

enough   —keşke—

          constellate this :

trouble   memory :   skewed

     uneven   prayer

       flags
if   —she—
    will

you mean, will   *you*

who long   *for—*

      "that view"

is not—

         what follows

here is a ritual   —she—   dares

      divine   what   practice

        happens   next—
    —she—

breaks   all   her—

        vows

no   thing
        precious

        —she—

    one   wish
              do not turn
              do not listen
              do not smile
              do not respond
              do not want—
              do not
    "stop"

İstiklal Caddesi

Can you name every girl you've kissed? You write this down so you won't forget
to ask next time.

List yours on the back of a Turkish Airlines boarding pass, astonished at columns,
forgetting and remembering in ballpoint.

There's another list, too, longer than you thought—
a surprise, really, the picture posted now five years old —it's starting to show, you said.

Cycle of 'account for.' Cycle of causality.

Yes, things that happened long ago. Still matter : boxes in a garage in California, pieces
of languages you knew now words (mostly nouns). A certain mouth rhythm.

You don't know the past tense for *keşke*: wind for hair or shapes for words. How you—
liked the sound of the call to prayer when it all came down to—

The horrible dress you would not have wanted to wear. Past conditional. Past
continuous. *She was waiting.*

Now : again the Bosphorus: this channel, this throat, choked city.
Wait here for no one. Even the textile man will not remember your name.

Why should you taste like kalecik karası when, by all accounts, you don't drink wine? You
watch the ferries come and go. Swoop of swallow, plum tree against old stone.

Tonight (tense change): you will put on a dress and dance on a rooftop and you will kiss
a man you do not love, who probably loves you, and you will wish it would've been—

Keşke VI.

—she—

     dawns

pink-washed   pale

     leaves

the city—

        sleeping   streets

garbage and glass   still blue

Bosphorus   sullen *simit* sellers

resting   architecture   forms

    çay drenched   before

      sun

       breaks

nights hold on—

    hours—stretch thin

  light

expands   contracts

—heart

       centers—

hunger

now familiar

      routes

again,   light   fills

              lack—

   exposes

what   will   not

   pass lips—

   —*keşke*—

   breath becomes

       the Ramadan light of June

   beneath

   will (as wish)—

shatter   this   fast

sea   absorbed

   light fades lavender

still   absent

                    words

empty   *words*

glass   *words*

        waits —

Keşke VII.

—she—   breaks

           away

from shore

           channels

open sea

receding

           : *focal plane* :

sea surface :   briefly broken

           gulls   beak

                     wing

past—   days of fasting

—she—   still :

           hungers

           empties

           the   small islands

pieces of candy

see :

nothing

left to break

—not line   not frame—

wishes are—

would   "you"

offer

sugar

cypress

crusted

Büyükada   ever

green

remember the old pine tree

tumbled

ruins—

stone house

—she—   imagines Greek

again

Calypso, the lustrous nymph

                    abandoned
—she—

        doesn't eat sweets any   way

        does not like   to wait—

bek   bek   bek   o bekliyordu

for every dive
                —resurface—
—she—

        spins sea foam

        into gold threads—

time   without
                —break—

keşke: breath

        of elma nargile

        of red achiote seeds

        of Pacific salt spray—

—she—   exhales   into

                        silence   fills

—Feast of Breaking—
                        —Fast—

Keşke VIII.

—she—

light soaked   stone

     color   sea

        gathered

     corners   a call—

a reggaeton beat

         rings

parchment   sky

         spills

     centuries   cement—

the woman locked in the tower—

           watched

           —longed—

I wish I did not have

           to leave more than you

    —O beautiful Balat of bad meals—

every surface   storied

     color   framed

     my heart is still

its name   show
    —me
     the seams

     — she—

connects   broken   repair—

Keşke sen hep gülsen
ben de seni izleseydim

    teach   me

    the word for my two—

     —keşke—

     —she—
    whispers   change

   sea   into   skin

    sink below

      salt   surface

      like a wish-

        tossed coin

Keşke IX.

—she—   returns

      sole   swallow

         another

point of origin :   **f/1.4**

                                      half

pine peaks   broken rock   face   *light gathered area*

south   Mediterranean

                          at midday :   wide blue lens

refracts   full   —she—   *relative brightness*

quickens   —*keşke*—   vast   field of view

        open   cave :   mouth

—she—   releases   breath   filtered

frame   azure   evergreen   eye—

                                        f/2

—light   pulls   taut

to mount—   *Olympos*

at 2 o'clock   still

sun   —she—   burns

body's   cruel   remnants—

remember :   April in July   Eliot—

          fragments   rock

ruin   sleeping

          sound   sea

stretched :   now

          silent :   now   blue—

                                        f/2.8

—light   reflections   float

4 o'clock   calm

here : no call   no voice

          collects

          small   stones

waves   wind   —salt spray—

pages

          turn

present   in absent

                form

—she—   ripples

the surface—

                              f/4
—light gathers   *length to*
        dragonspine   *diameter*
                    mountain

sun slips   6 o'clock
sea   softens   south—

Cyprus : Kyrenia, Nicosia—
        close—
                    point of other
        origin

her salt licked   skin
shuttered   around this
tightening circle—

                        f/5.6
vined terrace—frame
green—as *decreasing*
luminescence
            8 o'clock
shades —she— eats *patlican*
shrinks   time
        slows
—heart—   opens

so   let   so
much   moon
             rising

                         f/8
             red
half   drunk
 —she—
             sky
             lit
             star—

A Week After the Failed Military Coup

A week after the Failed Military Coup, you go south to Olympos. You're camped out with the book and all your *keşke*. Vine-covered. Ruins fallen into green river water. A week after the Failed Military Coup, some of your friends are banned from leaving the country. Word has just come through that you're exempt. You feel guilty for having worried over an upcoming trip to Scotland to celebrate your birthday. You meet Tarkin from Diyarbakır, who sells mussels on the beach, and you feel utterly alone for the first time in four years. You'll feel guilty for thinking about this, too. A week after the Failed Military Coup, broad-faced women in headscarves are making gözleme (*"observation"* — "do you remember — ?") that you eat on the beach. The Turkish Word of the Day is *insan hakları* — human rights. *Bahane* means excuse. *Korkak* means coward. He talks of Syrian refugees before he fucks you. The Failed Military Coup doesn't give you "perspective." You don't need prayers. A week after the Failed Military Coup, the water is warm. You think about *keşke* when you float — suspended in salt and sea — absorbing *differences in light transmission efficiency*. Code names. A week after the Failed Military Coup, Turkish words for "freedom" and "democracy" tattoo the headlines. You don't know the word for "disappointment" — or what is   inverse of —

— *keşke* —

Keşke X.

Rise

      this edge of—

greater length

          long

tumbled sea

        —her—

frame : the lone gull

a   cross   pages

      —she—

tears   so

all   names   sea

life   *—keşke—*   blown

a   part   borders

      this

        country

        blown

    off   course

the many currents

ruins   fragment   tossed

shells of—   cities :

              Gaziantep, Ankara, Diyarbakir, Mardin
deserts of—

          once   sea

crossed—   the countless refugees

now :   caravan

                 coastal plain
hunger   regrets

    cannot

    sail   a   way

war   wounds

    —keşke—

      if only

         words
mean—   less

         water

wishing   well: as   *—long—*

                  as
         grace
thresh

        holds—

Café Bien — Ankara

You pick Café Bien because it's close to your shuttle bus and his office.
It's been two days since the Kızılay bombing — *the evening of March 13*

rock music fills empty space : *a car laden with explosives* — he — *the third major attack*
shows you the broken windows of a friend's shop, *in Ankara in 6* — shows you his

stop — *killing at least 37 and wounding 125*, slivers glass eyes hollow, dark
where a number of bus lines meet men like him and not. Still you sit still

you sing because what else *officials failed to avert* will blossom
from scorched sound *sent burning debris showering down* into

silent *keşke*. You cannot stop looking at his hands. He said it was
close. He said he thought of you *a more naked form*

of terrorism reading about his death. *fire and heavily damaged* — you
say nothing you could say in his words. *According to an official statement* —

Because when your hands were cold, he took them,
an area a few hundred metres from the justice and interior ministries, a courthouse,

and the former office of the prime minister said how much
blood will fill this window this bus this woman this man —

pressed and sunken *the attack showed* more mouth than —
melting your body into. Fire, this thing we do *despite a number of*

intelligence warnings you know you'll remove that
later *Turkey's air force hit Kurdish rebel targets in northern Iraq*

Because candlelight appears less fully formed *the TAK: Kurdistan Freedom*
Falcons breath opens to — *claim responsibility for the attack*

salted air and acid jazz like that night in Izmir with Esen and Bilge, you
high on ecstasy and the world was amber and the stars in the dizzy sea

eyes dizzy now like then addiction and electric *the struggle against*
terror together that is all this and nothing more and all this and what

more, you said more the way he teaches you tongued deep
into pull of tidal law of physics — *"will for certain end"* –*keşke* —

    — *"will be brought to its knees."*

Keşke XI.

—she— knows

        dissent

                begins

     beneath

             as lie

thickest shades   feathered skies

     fallen

        fallen

light—

     wish   —a sentence—

     shadows

     water

say   has anyone ever told

say   think of this—

      flood   *You*

never know what is   *enough*

        unless
        you know
        what is   *more than*
        enough.
               —keşke—

—she—   discerns

      hungry clouds

measure   expanse

      formed

metals   cataracts of fire

light   and—

      how much I want

    —she—

      seas

more than—   visions   net

      golden threads

                Call me—. Call me—.

and it will be wonder—

cedar   *blood*

    lust

—full you say

    all

that is   not   action—

    —*keşke*—

failed   *if only*

prophecy   as

if   could   self

                  destruct

angels or

gods or

dreams or

                  imagination
could
        sing   one

                  wish—

—etched

Chiaroscuro in Valletta

Mark 6: 14–29
— AFTER CARAVAGGIO

Ask me. For anything: lightdark
dance deep down
dungeon dragged, need.

Measure me: volume of hip, hair
my soft shade—your hard
line—half
a kingdom for one
        crossed heart—

She : turns blood to dirt : she
turns and turns and—
        ask me for anything—

Break light
into shadow break
        me—girl—
gradiate me, murky

hold me to promise
        hold me—red—
            —down—
tight take me—tell me
        how *tenebroso*
will tell
        me—

Keşke XII.

—she—

      splits   stone

from wish   :   the Roman chapel

                ruins

belonging

                another

      one

condition   secures   absence

      holds   this

promise   no   one :

       to go
       to come
       to stay
       to leave

myth   or   memory :   *I might claim to be nothing less*
                                           than
      —she—
who   beckons   *—though you*

       might still wish—

"ben gidiyorum"

                              no

        hero

   holds   her

   back   words

              :

        from —   *you gods who cannot bear*

"to cover"   longing   *to let a goddess sleep with a man*

        even if—

it is   fate   *without*

        threads   *concealment*

and still :   "she that conceals"

skin   woven

        names

        rift

collapse   light

        aperture

what   we   leave out

—she—   *divine*

                         goddess

          binds

rock   to

     —*keşke*—

                    summons

          —gold

          —pacific

          —back lit

               caving—

Keşke XIII.

—she—
    crests
        and trenches
            where
is the matching stone

is the matching story

sea light—   windows   space

for more   breath   before

    flesh   there are 20 mountains
                                —Olympos—
    tracks   in the ancient world

sea floor :   *a dreamed role-pattern*

    open   heart
                   beats
one: question form :

two: will you

three: chain of—

four: *özür dilerim*—

five: *kötü bir gün geçiriyorum*

receive in —her

      şey   "you"

fail —   say *all right*

                say *please*

too   *much*   means

steady   say—

                        tiding

travels   the longing

                          distance

sea floor   :   a piece of Y in every X

             time

folds

        caves   secrets

            —she—

names   the crashing

      wait   :

      a balance

           against all that is

      her own

      escape   *"Çünkü . . .hep yanında çok mutluyum"*

        the sounding

call   —her—   *"Ceni ile birlikte hayat çok güzel"*

    yes   *"Eğer hayatlar böyle güzel*
          means   *yaşam varsa,*

     EVET,   what possible   *ben bu hayatı çok seviyorum*

so weave   mouth   to vines

sew trails   as departures as

       if

   cedar scent cleanly split

       could cut

          —her—
      in
        to—

A Month After the Failed Military Coup

A month after the Failed Military Coup, you're back on the southern coast, a year older. *Oh, for the love of . . . I was a coward! I was weak! I wouldn't—!* At Olympos Orange Bungalows, they learn your name. It's too hot to run, so you swim in the sea, returning to rhythms from other decades. *Astrid punches—.* The sea holds: a diaper, a used tampon, a replica pirate ship, small fish that bite your feet if you stay still long enough (this is not a metaphor), so many spectrums of light, you—*keşke.* A month after the Failed Military Coup, the Turkish Word of the Day is *bedava*—free (as in *gratis*, not *libre*). As in *iki tane alana, bir tane bedava.* As in, buy democracy, get dictatorship for free. You finish the book as the binding falls apart. *It's twelve days north of Hopeless*—860 pages of postmodern American poetry between you and the Failed Military Coup. *Everything we know about you guys is wrong.* The dinner bell rings at 20:00. *[she drops the butt of her axe on his chest] And *that's*—.*Your alarm rings at 09:00. 18:00 is 8 a.m in California.—*for everything else!* You know enough Turkish to know that most people mostly talk about—. *Dragon classifications: Strength Class, Fear Class, Mystery Class.* All conversations always begin with— *[about the dragons].* You are constantly, insistently— *This reclusive dragon inhabits sea caves and dark tide pools. What happens to the leftover food? Do you live here?* You tell yourself that you sing along so you don't forget the sounds of America but it's the sound of your own voice you're afraid of forgetting. *I do not want rice.* The country is in a 3-month State of Emergency. You have been sober for 11 days. *Extremely dangerous, extremely dangerous . . . kill on sight, kill on sight, kill on sight . . .* This might be a metaphor. *Never engage this dragon.* State of Emergency means—*Your only chance: hide and pray it does not find you—*

Keşke XIV.

—she— holds

    this
              photograph no one took :

    evidence

        dissolving

the particular :   wing of gull

over   *blindness of water*

Helsingør in August :   leeward where

castle walls   *words, words, words*

—she—   cannot speak

there is no blue as blue
        North

    wards

      —she—

    apparitions

ancient   art

of phantom   mourning

map   and   memory

you didn't—

           know

this moment   refuses

     translation

     how

Danish summer sun   lush

     light changes lyric

in   to   want

         —*keşke*—

ringed around castle

     crenelated

           —still—

wind   whisps

long sea   grass   reaching

    a   hand   *shored*

    against your   *ruins*—

later　　—she—　　will remember :

his speech　　　　stops

　　　only

　　　　　as

　　　　　—she—

　　　　　appears—

Keşke XV.

—she—

      rivers

the continent—   nymphs

the many banks and slopes

collect   :   *thy orisons*

      words so sweet of breath

rosemary   fennel   columbine

      rue

      pressed   dry

      between   pages

      —she—

burns   *remembrances*

no   —she—   thinks

      everything

      long longed—

Danube   Mosel   Rhine—

      take these again

      across the Baltic

where garlands wear—

      out

Northern seas or

      wilted prayers—

      words
             become
             rivers
      mad

river song   —she—

      translates

one final   grief

      —she—

will not cure—

will not silence

      form

into wide mouth   where

river is—

    sea

broken

—*keşke*—
          —waves
words
        denuded

    —she—   tosses

    away

blossoms   sea-scored

    rings of
        river
echo in your halls

her breath— *be*

    all your

    sins

    rememb'red

Keşke XVI.

—she—
       salt

       less

shape   shifting

       river   nymph—

       ruins

empire
       of—

       red   where red

meets river   blood

burnished—

—she—   affective aperture :

               water   river

               old   stone

               city   island

light box

   —she—

  chases   seas

  shadow   stone

    words

    other

fallen empires:

  church bells

  counter
spell   exposure
  time

take this picture :

colonnaded, the Roman baths—

—she—   dives

   deeply

minerals geology

  all

effects of affect—

      dissolve

  diameter   distance

      dissolve

sea blasted stone

        nymph

Maria—her empire—

      and all the many Marias—

          pray for us sinners   *now*
                                        and
          in the hour of our—

need
      —she—

emerges   wet

        skin—

Keşke XVII.

In the wet

      aftermath

—she—

         rushes

         brown

         beneath
the river

      drinks

rain or   slate

         white
wine

    —she—   turns

to water : a green lexicon

here : silence

missing sea

stone   fruit

      ripe

air : apple skin

   —she—

inhales claims

   —her body—

      rivered

towards distant
      seasons

affect   wrapped

breath   body's

temperature   drops

   rise   again

   rain—   patterned

river   moves through

   wake of—

    absence

refuses   embankment

refuses   soil

   ground

into this—

abandoned terroir of—

meanwhile

—she—

52 Albany St.

I've never been very good at being consistent. What are you most consistent at
is a question you can't answer. Through the window, seagulls—

Two days before your 36th birthday, the Turkish Word of the Day: *hastası olmak:*
to be crazy about. On 52 Albany St., you *tilt the camera to portrait mode; hold it*

extremely close. St Andrews Square: fairy lights in gin. On the day before—
the Turkish Word of the Day is *birisini ekmek*—to stand someone up.

I want to capture—, but landscape mode does not seem relevant here.

You're still thinking about macro mode to only have *that super narrow slice—*
Fruitmarket Gallery—where you didn't see the Mexican artist from D.F—

—and don't get me started on Mexico City—at midnight and all that
bullshit and the Turkish Word of the Day—your birthday—

is: *gerçek:* truth. You wonder about plurals—
True or False embrace just— half -truths.

True: you're still holding— *keşke.* False: *I have almost no light.*
Tutkulu bir fotoğraçıyım shows up a few days later: *I'm a passionate photographer—*

True: you always almost say— . You change the reservation anyway. Because
there are no candles, you forget to wish—what would have been— *keşke*—

When you wake up the next day, *a foamy wave reaching towards the lens*
the Turkish Word of the Day looks like: "His: Feelings." False—

Sample sentence: *Hislerimiz hakkında konuşmamız gerek.*
—We need to talk about our feelings— *but the endless sea and darkening sky—*

It's 10:36 a.m. on a Tuesday in August and at 52 Albany St. the rain
falls softly and softly falls upon all the Northern Renaissance

stone and you—   still don't understand alliterative verse or
how to talk about whiskey or where to go

next—

Keşke XVIII.

—she—   maps

time

worn   coast   lines

the   known world :   alluvial

Ottoman   *Admiral Piri Reis*

stories   *1521*

rivers   distant   drawing

seas :   secret bays   *oldest known*

surround Simena—   *Turkish*

—Kaleköy—

—she—

climbs   castle walled   *atlas*

into wild *kekik, adacayı, nane*   *to show*

stone   split   *New*

400 years   *World*

before   Christ—

the earthquake   sinks   Simena — Kekova :

          ships   *Caravola*—

    where   —Lycian

    Aegean   currents

                    Mediterranean
    broken   rocks

                    words   translate

Kekova island   :   *kekik, zeytin, limon var*

ama—

          he is bored of *tavuk şiş*—

remember recall repeat

          a name cut in half

                    Roman

    remains   beneath

          —she—

submerged

          —*keşke*—

sweet   sea   grass

          weaves

               kisses   *Uçağız : three mouths*

later she reads   *mouths*   means   three

                              open
                                   exits
                                             to sea—

68

Keşke XIX.

—she—   joins

        Mediterranean to Aegean

in Demre where the huntress

        wild and tame   *Artemis*

                refuses   *Lycian*

marriage   :   river to

sea   silt   covered   *alliance*

        Myra   worships

        Roman   *Diana's*

templed shadows :   *wilderness*   *virginity*   *childbirth*

        beneath   *moon*   *hunt*

        high   cliffs

        carved   rock   *belief :*

                tombs   *the dead*

resemble   treasure   *transported*

chests X marked   *by a wing—*

like   pirates map

               fabled   *like creature*

St Nicholas   his arrival

               steals

                        —her—

        star

nights sky :   Orion's bow

bends   sailors from Bari

—her—   heart   seize saint's

      forgotten   relics

Myra   in 1087

     heaps of *Murex* shells   purple dyed

          Andriake harbor at dusk

    —she—   *Artemis*

                    acted out in anger

           flies   *whenever*

from his boat   *her wishes—*

                        keşke—

        arrows   *disobeyed*

               seas

                  surfaces—

Neşko 1

You learn the rhythm by the third day. Eray raises and lowers the anchor. Mehmet
drives the boat and—. "You write" —*keşke*—. Remember : *the sound of water.* Taxis

boat to boat. In the evening, he— *air haunted by the taste of salt*—Skin.
The sun sets portside. Grilled shrimp and rakı. How could we help having more than

enough —*keşke*—: Andriake harbor in the morning. You watch sea
turtles. Fish. Things spoken as—unspoken give us a way. You broke your

vow of sobriety to dance barefoot. *That green before green before green
we perceive as air.* Do you like American music? Your best

friend texts: "You are every music video ever." Why then—
On the 4th day, Roman ruins slide starboard—you wonder if you could—

come for days—The passengers mistake you for crew. *Neşko* named for his dead
grandfather. His father—dead when he was three years old. No, he doesn't—tell

you all about it : the old house, working the boat at 13, the uncle the drunk stepfather
who beats his mother who is angry today because he didn't come home

last night you slept on the boat. He wakes you early. The Turkish Word
of the Day is *nefis.* Part of speech : adjective : *Nefisti* — That was delicious—

You tell yourself that someday—
soon you'll learn past tense—

Keşke XX.

—she—   could sing

      this
           —sea—

for all time

      muse   many

                moments

change light   chant

      blue   green

               —she—

bows his boat

               masthead

         belongs

antiquity

         to—

     siren

song : open

         waves

swollen   mouth   swallow

     sailor : hero

                                    whole

                         —she—

heroes her own

             tale—

spins   lyric   epic

                              sea
spray in

              to   sail

—keşke—   winds
                 trades

hard rock   for—

             —tune   still   fate—

kader   :   beni buraya kader getirdi

where   —she— guides

             ship
                      between—

             shape : coastal olive trees

             shift   green—grey—silver

                 —her—

hands   steer   to

        ward

against   shore

    break   —*keşke*—

from words

      worlds

span   knots—

thread days

    turn

years   forms

    —she—

Keşke XXI.

—she—   orange blossoms

      that scent

Finike once Phoenicus or Phineka

      remembers 1923

a   cross   buried

cliffs Limyra   ancient

      trading
port   stories
      night

boats   light   chain

star   sea   cigarette

nouns without names

      to burn

      the dead

          red sky at night, sailors delight

—she— drinks rakı

clouding   deep as —

knife   scars   if   prisons months
                  is
—*keşke*—   *red sky in morning,*

sailors take warning   "I am not a lucky man"

—she—   writes this   too

late—   *"where is*

                for —keşke—

"now"   "you"   know   —she—

is   also—

                dangerously

close the window

close the light
                and
wish—
        me
                well—

On the Road to Demre

Pulse beats and heart—stop. Center: base of sternum.
Kumluca to Finike to Andriake—*run run run run*

—pause— *run*, after and for a day, your body thrums crest
and trench and *as for you who long for* meanwhile Olympos meanwhile

underway. A small slip of paper still—somewhere and this is what
you would say—   *What is your half-life?*

And you used the word *enchantments* but it's not the stars or the music or—
Two cold bottles of cheap white wine, the night sound of rivers frogs or—

On the road to Demre, the sea glass sea makes you sleepy —no—
Kalbimdeki bu, derdi uyutursun uyutursun demiştin . . .Unutamam seni,

Unutamam canım—You like a song whose lyrics you can't understand
and you don't need to know the words of the song to know *Unutamam*

about *keşke*. If it wasn't—, you'd give up and talk about mothers or
marriage or verb conjugations or growing tomatoes and somehow it would be—.

Today we are the tumbling rocks past Finike—oh—your coastline
scent: sea plants stale cigarettes beer and boat fuel and all that warm—

—wish—

why haven't we, btw—so tell me why you won't write
and tell me why you won't come to Istanbul
and tell me all the things you won't tell me

Keşke XXII.

—she—

    kindles

        some new intrigue

Septembers   sand   strewn

        inside the hollow cave
    —*keşke*—

weeps   four days :   *on the fifth, Calypso*

    as   "for you who long for"

    swallows

    rise

return   in   this version

    —she—

does   not   give   *I know my body*

not gracious this   :   *is better than hers*

—she—   messy :   re

        fuses

raft to iron   light   lengthened water

so   two words   become

this
          mouth—

full   water   fall   river bend   anyplace

water breaks rock

     —cataracts—

in   to   caves

         sudden

skin   between teeth—

after all,

words   measure
     words

remove
       —keşke—

capital cities

switch   power

roles   reverse
    time

lines or composition

      —she—   *queen of goddesses*

    no   witness   *went home*

    to   faith

"you"   set frame   picture it—

       on the fifth, Calypso

     —she—   *let him go*

wearing hot red circles

      soundless

        scores—

        cave mouth—

      bruised half-moons

        embrace

          empty

        —*keşke*—

Keşke XXIII.

—she—

    slips

        under

cover   *deathless ageless goddess*

    —keşke—

        after

affect: slant of eye

    swears   breath *glutted*

          I will not plot more

    mortal

diversion   distraction

here : a new valley

    deep

ruin   again

        rose

   dawn

   broken

silhouette　　　:　　　Finike marina

　　　ships　　　sails

　　　　　distant

now　　—she—　　routes

　　　coastal

caravan of gifts :　　*wine, water, robes*

"and so much else, too"

cliff　　　wish

face　　　Demre

　　　silence

ending　　　:　　　"yes

I am happy　　yes

I am sure"
　　　　　—she—

lies　　between　　*what*

is　　near　　far

a　　way　　Ankara

or—   *this*

dream valediction :   "I am always here,

                                                    waiting"

            bana bak

            bana bakma   "But—"

—she—

      looks

      dissolving

                  —*keşke*—

this : sea   salt   wind

      pillared   wish

Two Months After the Failed Military Coup

Two months after the Failed Military Coup falls during The Feast of Sacrifice. It is the final day of Eid al-Adha. *101 So We gave him the good news of*—You're on your way to Copenhagen—*a boy ready to suffer and forbear.* The first day of the feast *the 10th day of Dhu al-Hijjah* was Monday *lasts for four days* and *begins with a prayer of two rakats* you were in Finike *followed by a sermon (khutbah).* On the first day of the feast, the Turkish Word of the Day is *fikir*—idea. *Sana bunun neden kötü bir fikir olduğuna dair bir düzine sebep gösterebilirim.* I can give you a dozen reasons why this is a bad idea. Because he went to say the prayers for his dead father—inverted sacrifice. When you ask, he—*an act of submission to God's command.* It's the only night he refuses to drink. *It honors the willingness of*—He leaves the feast to be with you *to sacrifice*—. He tells you the story of the stowaway cat. He tells you the story of how Hayrettin passed the breathalyzer. He tells you the story of the terrorist, the Molotov cocktail and his flaming uniform *before God then intervened sending*—. If you want to know more, you'll have to ask *thus indeed do We reward those who do right.* His first day in prison was his birthday (4 July). You don't speak of archangels. You don't use future tense. But "winter I come there"—*if Allah so wills. The meat from the sacrificed animal is divided into three parts.* Demre, Simena, Finike. Google translate. *Yoğun* means intense. *The family retains one third of the share* this night you don't turn on the music. This night another close *given to relatives, friends and neighbors.* In the morning, he *the remaining third* leans against the balcony *given to* smoking as sunrise over the marina. You snap the camera *poor and needy* but *"Thou hast already fulfilled the vision!"*—The first day of Eid al-Adha is the last time you'll see him *106 For this was obviously a trial*—. You run after him before the elevator door but—*107 And We ransomed him with a momentous sacrifice* you hold back—*keşke*—. You won't remember it anyway. Across the continent, you carry *Neşko 1*, the tumble-down streets of Demre at night, and the six hours in the Anadolu Hotel (before you're kicked out for not being married). Two months after the Failed Military Coup, the Turkish Word of the Day: *suçlamak*: to blame—*keşke*—. Two months after the Failed Military Coup, you learn that the government has decreed that Turkey will no longer practice Daylight Savings Time. *108 And We left (this blessing) for him among generations (to come) in later times:* Suspended in summer, you will not Fall Back, oh—you—will not Spring Forward.

Keşke XXIV.

—she—   remembers

                  words as

                                  sleep :

broken   by

                  gone   units

measure : long   Danish light   in

hair—   *strand* means beach—

             Aarhus coast

                or Roskilde—

                see the Viking ships

suspended   midair   —she—

swallows   flight   or—

                        I will not leave you to go

instinct   nest   for   air

blood for   —*keşke*—

far   away   Finike

                 to Demre :

    "must"   memory and—

            —she—

once   pacific   grace
                     crossed

continents of—
               holding

river   lake   canal   —sea—

the many moments
               thread
               time

loomed and spun   over

               distance

equals   —*keşke*—   so   turn

up   welling

wonder   waste
     land

    here
             and he doesn't like cats

ordinary   magic   or   other

wise   —she—   casts

                                      off

          ink

                    page

                    clothes

                                      shore

          no more—   lines

spell   —cave—

          bound   —her—

                          never

                                      once

                                      upon

                          ever

                                      after

                          all

Keşke XXV.

As the hills
                  fall
                        again

worlds recede : ridge : the greening

days form hours

                  plaited

                        desires — she —

not yet stone nor
                         — seas —

leave   taking   nothing

                        in   to

shored   treasures

               divine
                          what

simply   — she —   will

become twice

three   four   five

times

more

is—   error   slip

knot   tight

the final   breeze

harbors

broad back or risen spine

Teke peninsula

stretch   *West of—*

Taurus mountains

Kale   *renamed in 2005*

Demre

lies between   brown valleys

past   perfect

tense

the halyard   —she— had   longed

lined : crease of flesh

worn   grief

    sadness   a   wakes

    —keşke—   bow

raises

    —she—   nymphs

  skin   so

    briefly

—seven years or seven days—

    smuggled

    cave or ship

wait to— guide me

        bide—
forgive   this

wish   fills   Kaleköy's ancient cistern

    space   cannot hold

pleads   one   more

    time

NOTES

~ EPIGRAPHS ~

From Jack Spicer's poem, "Any fool can get into an ocean..."

From Charlie Anne's poem, "Myths and Female Bodies."

~ KEŞKE I ~

: the words in italics are taken from Robert Fagels' translation of Homer's *The Odyssey* (Books I & 5).

: "Words, words..."
Hamlet in Shakespeare's *Hamlet* (Act 2, Scene 2).

: "Be not deceived if I have veiled my looks"
Brutus in Shakespeare's *Julius Caesar* (Act 1, Scene 2).

~ KEŞKE II ~

: sing to me, what's left :
fragments from Robert Fagels' translation of Homer's *The Odyssey* (Book 1).

: San Juan :
San Juan Capistrano, a town in southern California known for the mission built by the Spanish and for the swallows which return to nest every year.

: now I seem to find her, now I realize / she's far away :
fragments from Petrarch's "Sonnet 227".

: sing to me, what's left :
fragments from Peter Riley's "Sing to me" (81.9) from *Book Two: This Carol They Began That Hour*: "sing to me, what's left of me"

: for how else can we invoke :
fragments from Mimi Khalvati's *Entries on Light*: "for how else can we invoke / after-worlds without / voice, light / but through things that // breathe and move, obey / an absence / that is deified because / absence is unbearable unless, in a residue / of breath and light"

~ KEŞKE III ~

: Lycia :
ancient geopolitical region comprised of the present-day Turkish provinces of Antalya, Burdur, and Muğla.

: Tahtalı Dağı :
Timber Mountain (Turkish)

: what were the right ways :
fragments from John Ashbery's poem, "Opposition to a Memorial": "What were the rights and the right ways"

: what was the name that you gave her? :
from Rosmarie Waldrop's poem, "We Will Always Ask, What Happened?"

: Zenicetes :
the pirate who ruled the city of Olympos from around 100 — 78 BC, when he was defeated by the Roman commander Publius Servilius Isauricus (and a young Julius Caesar). Unwilling to surrender, it is said that Zenicetes set fire to his own house and died.

: Yanartaş :
flaming rock (Turkish)

: emerge from rock / burn a flame that does not die by day or night :
from Pliny the Elder's description of Mt. Chimaera in the second book of *Historia Naturalis*.

: Χίμαιρα :
Chimera (Greek)

: enraged Anteia / dishonored / Bellerophon who / broke the sacred bond between /guest and host

: from *New World Encyclopedia*'s entry on
"Chimera (mythology)" :
https://www.newworldencyclopedia.org/entry/Chimera_(mythology)

: Anteia :
In Homer's telling, she was the wife of King Proetus of Argos who fell in
love with Bellerophon. He rejected her.

: Bellerophon :
Greek hero who survived many attempts on his life after Anteia falsely
accused him of adultery to her husband, the King of Proetus. Many of
Bellerophon's trials took place in Lycia. In Euripides, Bellerophon tames
Pegasus and fights the Chimera.

: witness these details :
fragments from Keith Waldrop's poem, "A Shipwreck in Haven (I)" :
"Witness these details. Your judgment, my / inclination. Hear. Touch. Taste.
/ Translate. Fixed: the river."

: Mount Omurga :
Mount Spine (Turkish). 3-peaked mountain located in Olympos, Turkey.

: Çamoda Peak :
one of Mount Omurga's distinctive peaks.

: Çıralı :
tiny coastal village next to Olympos. Considered to be the site of the ancient
Chimera due to the permanent gas methane vents on the mountainside that
produce flames.

: geography of /snakes from her :
fragments from Joan Retallack's poem, "Present Tense: Choice": "reconfig-
ure the geometry of attention in order to comb / the snakes from her hair"

: one solid braid
of sound— :
from Fanny Howe's, *The Wedding Dress: Meditations on Life Word*.

: wet, cool, bruises and might have been / care avoidance :
fragments from Paul Blackburn's, "Park Poem": "It is wet and cool / bruises
our skin / might have been / care and avoidance / but we run . run"

: plaited into desires not :
fragments from John Ashberry's poem, "The Skaters": "So error is plaited
into desires not yet born"

95

: will you read what / now reads :
  fragments from James Schulyer's poem, "The Crystal Lithium": "Other's
  eyes in the hope the other reads there what he reads"

~KEŞKE IV~

: a space you haven't yet filled :
  fragments from Nada Gordon and Gary Sullivan's poem, "Among the
  Living": "Because I reads your absence / in the space you haven't yet filled"

: before you tumbl'd me :
  Ophelia to Hamlet in Shakespeare's *Hamlet* (Act 4, Scene 5).

: a document in madness :
  Laertes in Shakespeare's *Hamlet* (Act 4, Scene 5).

: *you who long for things*:
  fragment from Brenda Hillman's poem, "First Tractate".

: she dreams that she speaks / the lines of the sea :
  from Laura Moriarty's poem, "Spectrum's Rhetoric".

~KEŞKE V~

: you who long for :
  fragment from Brenda Hillman's poem, "First Tractate".

~İSTIKLAL CADDESI~

: İstiklal Caddesi :
  main street in the center of Istanbul, Turkey.

: *kalecik karası* :
  varietal of Turkish red wine.

~KEŞKE VI~

: *simit* :
  type of Turkish bagel commonly sold by street vendors.

: *çay* :
  tea (Turkish)

: words words words :
Hamlet in Shakespeare's *Hamlet* (Act 2, Scene 2).

~KEŞKE VII~

: Büyükada :
a small island in the Bosphorus off the coast of Istanbul.

: Calypso, the lustrous nymph :
from Robert Fagels' translation of Homer's *The Odyssey* (Book 1).

: *bek* :
wait (imperative, Turkish)

: *o bekliyordu* :
she was waiting (Turkish)

: *elma* :
apple (Turkish)

~KEŞKE VIII~

: Balat :
a neighborhood in Istanbul.

: *Keşke sen hep gülsen / ben de seni izleseydim* :
I wish you always smile / I would watch you, too (Turkish)

~KEŞKE IX~

: Kyrenia, Nicosia :
Cities in the divided island of Cyprus in the eastern Mediterranean. Nicosia
is the capital of the Republic of Cyprus (Greek). Kyrenia is a coastal port
town in the Turkish occupied Turkish Republic of Northern Cyprus (TRNC).

: *patlican* :
eggplant/aubergine (Turkish)

~KEŞKE X~

: this edge of greater length :
fragments from Kathleenn Fraser's poem, "re: searches (fragments,

after Anakreon, for Emily Dickinson": " not random, these / crystalline structures, these/ non-reversible orders, this / camera forming tendencies, this / edge of greater length, this / lyric forever error, this / something embarrassingly clear, this / language we come up against"

: Gaziantep, Ankara, Diyarbakir, Mardin :
cities in Turkey.

~CAFÉ BIEN–ANKARA~

: the italicized text is taken from Constanze Letsche's March 14, 2016 article in *The Guardian*, "Ankara car bomb: Turkish president vows to defeat terror after dozens killed."

~CHIAROSCURO IN VALLETTA ~

: Valletta :
capital city of Malta.

: tenebroso :
in art, a term used to describe a style of dark and obscured painting that uses shadow and light. Caravaggio is known for his use of this technique.

~KEŞKE XII~

: the italicized text is taken from Robert Fagels' translation of Homer's *The Odyssey*.

: *ben gidiyorum* :
I am going (Turkish)

: "to cover" and "she that conceals" :
Greek translations of the meaning of Calypso (Καλυψώ).

~KEŞKE XIII~

: a dreamed role-pattern :
fragments from John Ashberry's poem, "Paradoxes and Oxymorons":
"A deeper outside thing, a dreamed role-pattern / As in the division of grace these long August days."

: *özür dilerim* :
I'm sorry (Turkish)

: *kötü bir gün geçiriyorum* :
I'm having a bad day (Turkish)

: *"Çünkü...hep yanında çok mutluyum"* :
Because I am always so happy with you (Turkish)

: *"Ceni ile birlikte hayat çok güzel"* :
Life with Ceni is beautiful (Turkish)

: *"Eğer haytlar böyle güzel yaşam varsa, EVET, ben bu hayatı çok seviyorum"* :
If there's such a beautiful life, then, yes, I love this life so much (Turkish)

~A MONTH AFTER THE FAILED MILITARY COUP~

: the text in italics is taken from the script of the film, *How to Tame Your Dragon* (2010, Dir. Chris Sanders & Dean DeBlois, Paramount Pictures).

~KEŞKE XIV~

: this photograph no one took / evidence :
fragments from Michael Palmer's poem, "Of": "Of this photograph no one has taken" & "This photograph no one has seen / offers itself in evidence"

: blindness of water :
fragment from Paul Blackburn's poem, "El Camino Verde": "wing of gull over blindness of water"

: Helsingør :
city in Denmark, setting for Shakespeare's *Hamlet*.

: words, words words :
Hamlet in Shakespeare's *Hamlet* (Act 2, Scene 2).

: "shored against" "ruins" :
fragments from T.S. Eliot's, "The Wasteland": "These fragments / shored against my ruins"

~KEŞKE XV~

: the italicized text is taken from Ophelia's words to Hamlet in Shakespeare's *Hamlet* (Act 3, Scene 1). The final line is a slightly modified version of the last line of Hamlet's famous soliloquy in Act 3, Scene 1.

: Danube, Mosel, Rhine :
rivers in central Europe.

~52 ALBANY ST.~

: the italicized English text are fragments from a July 29th 2016 post on "Analog Anecdotes," a blog by Péter Levay: https://analogans.wordpress.com/2016/07/29/sliced-up/#more-322

~KEŞKE XVIII~

: Simena, Kaleköy, Kekova, Caravola:
Ancient Greek and Turkish names for a coastal city in southwestern Turkey, on the Lycian trail.

: *kekik, adacayı, nane* :
oregano, bay leaf, mint (Turkish)

: *kekik, zeytin, limon var* :
there's oregano, olives, and lemon (Turkish).

: *ama:*
but (Turkish)

: *tavuk şiş* :
grilled chicken skewers (Turkish)

: Uçağız :
village next to Kaleköy, named for its three bays.

~KEŞKE XIX~

: the italicized text is taken from the entry on Artemis from "Greek Gods & Goddesses": https://greekgodsandgoddesses.net/goddesses/artemis/
and David Goran's June 9th 2016 article in the *Vintage News*, "The ancient Lycian ruins of Myra are breathtaking and highly unusual in appearance."

https://www.thevintagenews.com/2016/06/09/ancient-lycian-ruins-myra
-breathtaking-highly-unusual-appearance/

: Demre :
coastal city in southwestern Turkey, formerly known as Kale in Turkish and
Myra to the ancient Greeks. It is believed to be the burial site of St. Nicholas
and is a pilgrimage destination for many Roman Catholics and Eastern
Orthodox Christians.

: Myra :
site of ancient Greek ruins outside the city center of Demre, known for its
rock-cut tombs. Legend says that the tombs were built high in the cliffs
so that the dead could be transported to the underworld by a wing-like
creature.

: Bari :
Adriatic town in southern Italy. It is believed that sailors from Bari stole the
sacred relics of St. Nicholas from Demre in 1087.

: Murex :
generic Latin name for a type of sea snail. Ancient Phoenicans and Jews
harvested murex for purple dye.

~NEŞKO 1~

: come for days :
fragments from Aaron Shurin's Involuntary Lyrics,"CII": "if you would come
for days"

: air haunted by the taste of salt :
from Thom Gunn's poem, "Confessions of the Life Artist".

: That green before green before green / we perceive as air :
fragments from Julie Carr's poem, "Of Sarah": "That green before green
before green, that roundness we perceive as air"

~KEŞKE XX~

: kader :
fate (Turkish)

: beni buraya kader getirdi :
fate brought me here (Turkish).

~ KEŞKE XXI ~

: Finike :
a coastal town in southwestern Turkey, called Phoenicus or Phineka by the
Greeks.

: 1923 :
the year of the population exchange between Greece and Turkey.

: Limyra :
a small city in ancient Lycia, on the southwestern coast of Turkey.

: *rakı* :
anise-flavored alcohol, similar to ouzo (Turkish).

~ ON THE ROAD TO DEMRE ~

: Kumluca :
coastal town in southwestern Turkey.

: Andriake :
Demre's harbor.

: you who long for:
fragment from Brenda Hillman's poem, "First Tractate".

: *Kalbimdeki bu, derdi uyutursun uyutursun demiştin . . .*
Unutamam seni, Unutamam canım :
"This is what's in my heart, you said you would make me sleep . . .
I can't forget you, I can't forget dear" (Turkish), from lyrics to the song,
"Unutamam seni" by Koray Avcı.

~ KEŞKE XXII ~

: the text in italics is taken from Emily Wilson's translation of Homer's *The
Odyssey*, Book 5.

: "for you who long for" :
fragment from Brenda Hillman's poem, "First Tractate".

~KEŞKE XXIII~

: the italicized text is taken from Emily Wilson's translation of Homer's *The Odyssey*, Book 5.

: *bana bak* :
look at me (imperative, Turkish)

: *bana bakma* :
don't look at me (imperative, Turkish)

~TWO MONTHS AFTER THE FAILED MILITARY COUP~

: the italicized text in English is taken from the Qur'an. The Qur'an, *As-Saffat* 37.101-108.

: Eid al-Adha :
Muslim feast day/holiday celebrating the willingness of Abraham to sacrifice his son, Isaac.

~KEŞKE XXIV~

: Aarhus :
coastal town in Denmark.

: Roskilde :
coastal town in Denmark, known for its Viking museum (and rock festival).

~KEŞKE XXV~

: Teke peninsula :
peninsula located between Antalya and Fethiye in southwestern Turkey.

: Taurus mountains :
mountain range in southern Turkey separating the Anatolian plain from the Mediterranean coast

: Kale :
former name for Demre, a city in southwestern Turkey.

ACKNOWLEDGMENTS

Poems (and versions of these poems) appeared in the following publications: *Gyroscope, Panoply, Versal, The Drowning Gull, New Delta Review, Glass Poetry Review, The Poets Billow, Sliver of Stone, Read Water* anthology by Locked Horn Press, *Placeholder Magazine, Inverted Syntax, Alternating Current, Paris Lit Up, Interim: A Journal of Poetry and Poetics, Mediterranean Poetry*

Teşekkür ederim :
~ Gökhan Özdemir for teaching me the one word for my two ~
~ Heather Yeung, who told me keşke was a book ~
~ everyone who talked to me about photography during 2016 ~
~ Olympos Orange Bungalows ~
~ the crew of Neşko 1 (2016–2018): Mehmet, Eray, Hayrettin, Mert, Salih ~
~ Ali, who sold me a ticket for a boat ride, and Elena, for taking me under her wing ~
~ the folks at the Turkish Word of the Day ~
~ the editors of all the outstanding journals who selected pieces of this project for publication ~
    ~ particularly Anna Arov and Megan Garr and the crew at *Versal* for the Utrecht reading and for their advice, and for doing work that matters ~
    ~particularly Stephanie Papa at *Paris Lit Up Magazine* for the thoughtful edits to 52 Albany St.~

~ my friends who listened, read drafts, collaborated and offered opinions: Michael Subialka, Jessica Stillman, Molly Williams, Kat Sanchez, Péter Levay ~

~ Bilkent University, for funding me during the initial writing of this manuscript

  ~ particularly Prof. Dr. Mehmet Kalpaklı for his gracious enthusiasm for poetry (and carpets) (and wine) ~

~ my family, for their support and encouragement

  ~ particularly Charlotte, who has been siren and sailor both ~

~Memo: *Evet, mutluyum. Evet, eminim.* ~

~ and Gonzalo, the shore to my sea.

Airlie Press is grateful to the following sponsors and individuals, whose contributions provided major support in funding this and other Airlie Press books of poetry.

Joelle Barrios

Joanie Campf

Jane Comerford

Chip Ettinger

Cecilia Hagan

Quinton Hallett

Dennis Harper

Donna Henderson

Hannah Larabee

John Laurence

Karen McPherson

Alida Rol

Kat Sanchez

ABOUT THE PUBLISHER

Airlie Press is run by writers. A nonprofit publishing collective, the press is dedicated to producing beautiful and compelling books of poetry. Its mission is to offer a shared-work publishing alternative for writers working in the Pacific Northwest. Airlie Press is supported by book sales, grants, and donations. All funds return to the press for the creation of new books of poetry.

COLOPHON

The poems are set in Merope, courtesy of Tseng Information Systems.

Printed in Portland, Oregon, USA